THE HEX OF ZERO HOURS

THE SHADES OF PARADOX

SUMEET KUMAR

ISBN 979-888546131-3

Sumeeet Kumar

Sumeet Kumar , A adult who experiences many phases of love in his life , get broked many times , stands up every time and keep moving to the next phases of the life.In reality he is a writter as well as singer (as a hobby).

Very exciting and interesting fact about him is that he is aauthor of New era i.e. he starts his journey of writing at the age when he was going to schools to get the study.His some famous works i.e. Maturity Of Love (Genre - Love),Privacy For Dream (Genre - Middle Class), Army Squad ofLove (Genre- The Seperation of Army Love), 5 Days of Love(Genre- Temporarily Love), Th e Endearment Of Love(Genre - Historical Era Of Love), Social Destruction Indo-Pak (Genre - The Story of The Love At The Time Of Division Of India And Pakistan), Middle Class Soul (Genre - The Dreams of Middle Class), The Accursed Kanatpur (Genre -The Horrific Story Of A Village), Wrong Number (Genre -The Suspenseful Physco Killer Story), The Secrecy OfDeadly Midnight (Genre - The Suspense About a Crime),Fragile Religious Of Death (Genre- The Death Of A TrustfulPerson), Nature Vs Science (Genre - The Future Battle Between Nature And Science In A Horrific Way), Generic Man (Genre - The Dream of I.I.T), The Unconsious 12 Hours(Genre - The Illusion At Stage Of Comma), The StrangeBurden (Genre - The Burden Of Love) , Her Existence (Genre- The Female Pain In The Society) , Jockstrap Prize (Genre -The True Story Of A National Athlete) , H Man [Hindi] (Genre - Superhero Tragic Story), H Man [English] (Genre - Superhero Tragic Story) , Maturity Of Love [Englsih] (Genre - Love). are available on various geners on the offcial platform of Amazon, Flipkart and Notionpress. You can buy them from there.

Contents

ACKNOWLEDGEMENTS

Aman Kumar

Special Thanks to **Aman Kumar** who worked so hard
in the preparation of this book. He has continually put
with my passive voice, omission of words, and late night
calls. You have be en wonderful. Thanks to him for his
precious time in reviewing proposals , individual chapters
and early drafts, along with his suggestions on the

applicability of the material to the world.

I

The Scene Of HEX

This is a story whose beginning is also a mystery and the gut is also a mystery. If it doesn't work out, it's okay, if it doesn't come out, it will remain a mystery, according to the undefined time, if someone's truth turns out to be a fraud, then he also gets a reason to correct it, and the wrong crime is also known, which further It is going to be undefined that even a relationship has a lot of secrets, like a crime, undefined also has many secrets, it has many side effects and if that relationship is broken by mistake, then it has different secrets. This whole life is also a mystery somewhere in our life, there is a question, it is sudden and true, this is a crime which no one has ever committed. There are many characters in our life as well, I mean, behind a person's gross, there are many secrets, many masks, many different identities. Just like a crime also has many secrets, many problems and many different masks with many questions. This is a crime story of a male witness who buried his own death in his arms several times along with his own soul. That witness was murdered, but his questions were still chasing the male secret, due to which he had died. Seeing someone's silence, we find many predictions and reasons. But when such a face comes in front whose happiness does not know how many secrets of pain he has hidden inside himself, then later we can not even predict it. How many secrets of the country will there be? When someone's death happens suddenly, we also understand that it will be the will of someone above, but when even a splatter gets killed, no one says that there is absolutely someone's hand behind it, everyone understands that it is of nature. There is a game. But there is nature behind every witness, so it is not made by any human being in the world. No one's death is recognized by nature nowadays, but we never want to find the reason behind it. Rahashya Tohar Behind the death of a witness, whether he dies because of God's or human's. Well let's start with the mystery of such a death whose character is many but his friend is only one.

""Crime and mystery have a strange hiccups because they can't live without each other""

II
The Intro Of Survivor

Amsterdam, Satyaandparat WesternNetherlands was located to which Selmir and connected to the North. A city whose beauty is nowhere to be compared. But where there is beauty, its secrets are also enough. There lived a witness whose name was George, a cardiologist by profession, who has always been alone in Sehar because his mother and father did not live together since childhood as they were divorced in George's childhood when he was about 5 years old. He had felt so lonely from the happy time that later he made happy loneliness the reason for his life. Bash got everything in childhood except one thing which he needed all the time His life is his own soul, he asks him later this question that what is your identity, what is the means of living. Because he also changed his loneliness into a happy happiness whose secrets were not known to anyone except him. When George was 5 years old Since then he started living in Amsterdam because because of the divorce of his mother and father, he chose a destination where he got everything. Even though he had been alone since childhood, he found himself alone in the condition, he still never lost his silence. Somebody let the loneliness grow so that it might become the reason for his death later. K. Log loved him a lot. He loved himself too, due to which he never felt that silence. George was such a person The one who never had enmity with anyone, lived with everyone very lovingly, and never was envious of anyone and no one was jealous of him in his profession undefined those closest to him. Loved himself more at the time, Bash used to listen to what he said, George loved him more than his mother and father and he was all George's watchers who were from a Muslim family whose surname was Mirza, that too George Like his son, he believed that his son had also died in a car incident, because at that time George was so close to him that he never felt the memory of his son ... and more wires George leaving his own house He used to live in his house, whenever he went, he used to take him along with him. Although sometimes George used to support him in his financial problems too, due to the departure of his son, there was a lot of trouble in the beginning but when Jamalar Amirza got a company like this I got a job where his post was that of a watchman and he did this job thinking that maybe doing this job would improve the condition of his house. But he never even mentioned to them what work his beta did... the point where George was in the business of a cardiologist. While working, he met Ava, who was also a neurologist by profession. When they first met, George did not know him because even though he would help everyone all the time, he never had any relation with them undefined George While watching the report of a patient, only then a serious case came to the fore in which a police officer was shot 2 inches above the heart, a bullet was also hit in his hand. Due to which he had lost a lot of blood. There was a lot of need of that which was not in the hospital at that time, it came to know that someone in block 13 needs blood group, he met George even at that time George did not see him but when the police officer was saved in the aftermath. It was very difficult without Ava's blood group to save time. Then after the lucky time came out and the police officer's life was saved, George met Ava and said to Ava (You did the great job be saving someone) 's life, and thanks for your blood which saves him and make a miracle today.)

Conversation

""

George : *So , its George from the cardio department,*
What's your name

***Ava** : hello , it's me Ava from neurologist
department.
George : Nice to meet Ava.l want to say something
to you that you have born with a great smile and a
good healing heart.Can we go for a cup of tea???
Ava : Sorry, it's not possible today.If you will not be
busy tomorrow, so can we meet tomorrow ...
George : Yeah sure! why not.Ok we will meet
tomorrow at 10o; clock ...
Ava : Ok done, Byeee see you Tomorrow...*
„"

One day George did not know that meeting time is the biggest happiness of his life and also the reason for his death. Maybe he did not say that??? After that he met the next day and in a few words Ava said this to George. I love you when I saw you helping my child for the first time I wanted to say that you started liking me from the day but I felt that now is not the right time, so I have nothing at this time. But it is alpha toh silent Can stay but the feelings of my heart can't be silent for you..after that George said that I can't love anyone even after passing this time, I can't get into a relationship with anyone because I have full faith in everyone. No. I will stay with you, even if I loved you, I will not be able to handle it, but I can say that you are a very good girl, I do not deserve you .I'm sorry no such thing, not you toh bash you told me about my heart and nothing else. I'm fine ..ok leave it tell me you're here since childhood, it just came a few years ago because I've never told you before See... you are right, I have come home only a few years ago, I was in the Netherlands and I have completed my entire studies, only then I thought of doing neurologist....

after that I completed my full studies. and later when i got replacement then i came to amsterdam from netherlands... you tell me how you do this...???my childhood is like this i was 5 years old since then i am with my uncle..(At that time George did not want to tell anyone about your past, he shared all his things with the same family, before that it was Mirza family, so he did not know much about himself. I told. No more Ava asked him more... after that they talked for a long time then left.....

"" For helpless insects,
worms have also advanced to the present
day.."

III

The Recognition

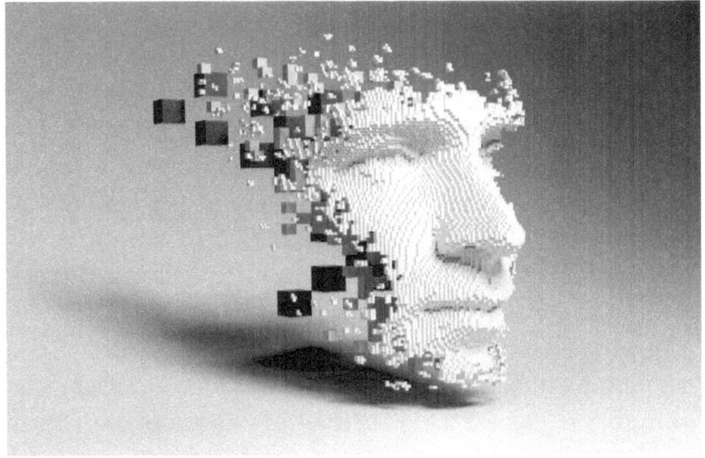

During this day they started meeting quite a lot with each other, but they never got the relationship that Manwa used to come with George. Another thing was that George loved his business very much and always paid attention to her. And most of the time he used to help such families, then they were normal but disabled. He also had an organization of his own, with the help of which he used to do all this work. Why don't you relate to it.. By the way, tell one thing, Dangeorge was born in India, a sehar named Bangalore, but because of your mother and father's divorce, he was sent to Amsterdam by his mother, he had enough professions that he could buy the entire Bangalore Was .. yet he chose such a sector so that he could help the people. By the way, her dad was also a cardiologist and she was a momek business woman who was quite a driver to take any household decision, none of this work was done without asking her. (They say no women's are the head of the house) Her talaq The only reason for this was that George's momkishi was in love with her and his father Aishethe who had already done two marriages. But the news of the marriage was never to George's mother. George Kasli was Sanat Kshatriya by the way and his Mother Kapurra's name was Palak Kshatriya and her father's name was Nurag Kshatriya.Suru Suru Her mother's father's relationship was with Kishore since George was not even born undefined George's father knew that Palkusse did not love anyone else but she never said anything to him because he himself knew that somewhere he himself is also wrong undefined Later it became because of George's grandfather, he was a big business of Bangalore undefined and he was his daughter-in-law. Considered the foster very much, cared for him a lot, so even at the time of his death, he gave assets in the name of his future child, I mean George. (name of a child who was not yet available). George's grandfather used to be very proud of his mother, only then the day he talked to the foster about all this, only a few days after that he had a heart attack due to which he died... The property was also given to Jorje's name as soon as the Puri property belonged to George's name and he was killed a few days later. Why didn't he save them???????It's a mystery after all and George's grandfather's reason for Kimrn's heart attack is because of him.

"

"Supposedly, the My veins told me about my
death,
because what she considered her sympathizers
turned out to be the same Waste...."

IV
The Eye Of Evil Planniing

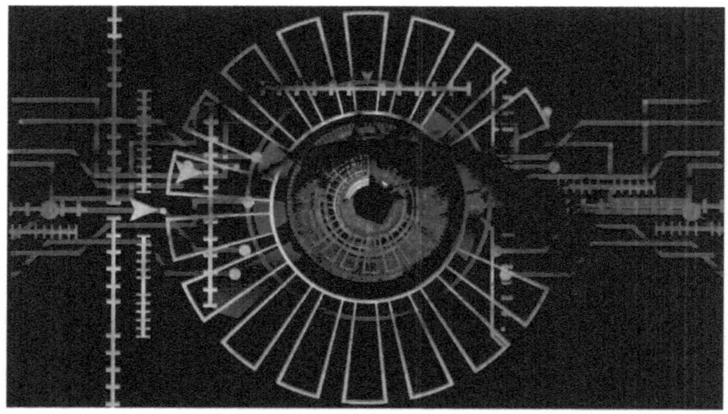

The time when the parent was called by George's grandfather, or who had shown the bakest paper that he had made and had shown the name of someone other than George and that name was of Tarun because he thought that he was killed in Agra, then it is true. It will never come out that his another son may be illegitimate, but it is the blood of Kshatriya, that day he told everything about Anurag and about his padashree granddaughter and said that after my death, you all stay together only then you both have wealth. His son will be named. At that time, the parents happily obeyed him, but no one knew what he was going to do with them. Hearing this, she left in a short time and in a short time when the truth came immediately. And she also went away after meeting them undefined then only then the foster came again with her IG whom she loved and when they saw both of them together then only .. before they asked anything, Palkaur her lover Arjun accompanied her Together, they gave Mardia. They often added a cash drug named (Nasides) which would have been very dangerous for a patient and the reason for the most shocking is also undefined (everyone must have guessed that the thing was not detected in this report in the blood). It was not known when someone told the matter because he was involved in the murder of Dr. George's grandfather. That's why when Anurag asked this, then the male doctor told him that he died due to the decrease in oxygen level undefined if male. If Anurag had given a look to the reports, he would never have seen this day? And if George's grandfather had not trusted himself too much, then he would certainly not have died at all. After that her purri wealth was in the name of Jorge and Tarun but because of this she used to tell Palakatrun to die too but this time it could not happen because all the time Anurag used to stay with her Nahitoh Akashnath used to live with her due to which it was a bit difficult to kill her. And at the young time the foster was also pregnant, due to which she could not kill him. That's why he thought that when the time comes, she will kill him too. Then let him live till now... the deal of death was not over yet. Going forward, things will definitely happen with you in some way or the other. (Karma's name is Sunna, sometimes if it is Sunna from Kishi, then it means that if it is not then know then undefined, after a few months, she was pregnant, then it should have been 9 months. When he went, he had an accident in which his child was miscarrying and he died before birth. When it happened, Anurag was not with him at that time, due to which he and Arjun thought that now the surgery property will go away from us and its owner will only go to Anurag's son Tarun Baan. Take God instead of your son so that our property will not go away and the school will also get a rain

"*The Frog You Have Called***
His wish is the only way....
*Nothing else ...***"**

V

The Father Of Hell Comes

mhε gσ∂ σf нεℓℓ ¢σмεѕ συm

Did George's grandfather really die of a heart attack this day? Somebody had murdered him in the sack? That's when he had also said one more thing that if I die, then only my grandson will have the right on the surgery property and no one else, he will become the sole heir of my family, that is, after my departure, the same thing will happen to Merilegakay if by mistake he too. If death occurs, then only one person is the owner of the entire property, that is undefined to you, that is, the guardian, after the death of George, will be the owner of that entire property and no one else.) The parent was very happy to hear this because his father-in-law's entire property was going to be available... Gave? After all, what happened that he gave his sari property to a person who was not even his own, undefined Who is the right thing after all, undefined again the only mystery whose questions are many but the answer is one. The name is because he knew the truth about your son; Did you know the truth of the letters?

George's grandfather didn't have a heart attack but because he was a bimmer because he knew very well that his son had another wife and his Apart from the foster, there is another daughter-in-law and she also has two children. I used to love more but I didn't want to tell you because she is the daughter of your enemy. Who is the enemy?? Akash Nath you married Akash Nath's daughter and she didn't tell you anything. I'm sorry dad but he said that if you give me a tender with saffron in your company, then I will let you marry your daughter. That's why I went and gave all the tenders I had to her. Maybe go away from the marionazzos. I will take them in front .. then only after talking to them after talking a heart attack but goes and at the same time takes them to the hospital where they are deaf from danger but not from you. But what did they know that it is their own whom they love more than themselves, they have become such a big enemy in a few days that they are thirsty for their blood

"

"*Fact only my veins knows*"

what was the reason of my death............""

In the hospital where he is taken to the hospital, his own beta was a cardiologist doctor who operated on him himself. When he regained consciousness, he first called the foster and told all the things he had and then the best paparambiya in which it was clear. It was clearly written that he has given his entire property to his grandson. But this was not true, yet there is another such sack from whom the mask is still pending. A mystery that will be shocked to hear what happened. After a while, his son Anurag is also there with you son whose name was Tarun. What was the fault of the one who was only 3 years old. Anurag had apologized to him at the same time but he had forgiven him at the same time, but when Anurag came out from him for some time and when he again left his son at his house When he came back, his father was murdered at the time. He was not getting this thing from the society. His dad was fine, how it happened sometime back, when it happened, he started asking everyone, but everyone had only one answer that was the only one. Did it really happen that there is some confusion behind this too, the question is, who killed these people, who is the culprit behind their death.....then later all the society had taken that this is an incident only because of the above-mentioned kickjis. Now that god is not in the world.

VI
The Execution

Lawyer's death Arjun's going to jail was a close link between everyone, there was only one person behind all Arjun's worst habit was that every time you used to carry a knife with you and the day that lawyer was going to die before that he was the guardian. Had come to meet her at her house, then at the same time Anurag also came, seeing him, in a hurry, you put the knife on a desk, he had many stories about the disciple's mystery that she was in love with someone else and it was deceiving me. That's when she had come to ask him on this very day that he saw Arjun going inside and also numbed his bati. Then he very cleverly kept the dryness close by (because the first thing was such that he was with Arjuna) Mostly, Anurag had seen the knife with him several times) Only then Arjun and the foster did not realize that it was a knife. And before Arjun went to the lawyer, Anurag went and killed him. And he was wearing two gloves in his hands, because of which when Arjunwaha came, Anurag had said the same thing and he had already called the police from the landline. Had given that the lawyer sahib has died, now as soon as you have come home, then he will be furrarar. When the police, who are you and who will be farrarho, he had already disconnected the call. And when the police came in a while, he was present. On seeing Arjun, he considered him guilty and he was also the same, due to which the police got a proof against Arjun and when the police matched the finger prints of Arjun and Nishan on the wheel, then they started feeling that Arjun had killed the lawyer. Another thing was the lawyer had told everything to Anurag before he died that what he was going to do with your son and he showed you the Heglatt paper, due to which whatever property your father has, he should be his. Since then Anurag had realized He will do anything to save his son and he also kept a copy of the original bakest paper from him. Do not see because Vaijanta was that if she came to know that I am behind everyone, then she was neither left nor me. There was a reason for the family, due to which Anurag cleverly took divorce from the parent and told his whole truth to understand that I am already married, I have two children too, I find that I am not worthy of you now. I don't want to ask for anything, if possible please give me those things in your rights And legkay I don't want anything, keep all this for you, but there is a request that please move forward in life. All this, the parent started feeling that Anurag is not wrong, he only loves a person without whom it cannot live. And in the way Arjun Can't live without her, in the same way, Anurag also can't live without his first love. After all the debauchery that Anurag had played with his foster parents, he divorced her, due to which nothing happens to Voteroon. But one thing Still nagging that when Anurag can kill the lawyer then he should visit the foster He could have committed murder, but why did he do this at the time undefined Well after all the parents signed the divorce papers and finally they got divorced. But never tried to know the secret behind him..If Wash had tried a little while, Arjun would have been with him undefined Now Satya started feeling that he saved his son but did he really save it???? Was away from undefined They thought that he had died but it was not so, then who killed him, who killed him, who is to blame??????? In this story...........

**"*"All the time,*
*I have kept myself in my heart***

and others with compassion"”

THE END WITH A SMILE

Even though the destination is the last but the journey is not over yet.. 20th July, 2020 Today, when George was said to be 20 years old, and according to the best paper, the entire 70 parent owners also belonged to the Kshatriya legacy. This news was now known to everyone that George is now 20 years old. Which turned out to be his enemy. I had said earlier that there was no enemy of George in Amsterdam. But he had many enemies in Indian who were behind his life. That too because of his profession, George never knew this It was not that she is the owner of 70 parents. Because Palakne never told her this and how would she tell because it was clearly written in the Bequist paper that if for some reason George dies after 19 years, then it is in the name of his successor and Kshatriya Legacy Parent. Anurag's name will be there ... But George's grandfather did not know that the people who trust the most and love the most, the same log is thirsty for their blood undefined Now something was going to happen to George that no one expected. Her own mother did not. Palak had sent George to kill his own daughter who was none other than Ava. Undefined is Ava was his real daughter. Jishepalak had sent him to kill Ava was the daughter of both Arjuna and Palak, that too before marriage but not George K's grandfather did not know and neither did Anurag.. there was another reason behind killing George that if he died then Arjun would get bail.(But how would this undefined foster fool a judge whose speech and justice) She used to walk on money, she told the guardian that if you have given so many professions, then I will get Arjuna bailed out, it will be my responsibility to get him out of the case. So he waited for a long time, when George would be 20 years old, then I would kill him and take all the property in his own name. Could ask. And the foster felt that Arjun had killed Tarun before going to jail. Because he used to say that You are upset, I find some way out. She had sent Ava to kill George but she didn't let him die because she fell in love with him and she used to say whatever the mystery is, she has come to Amsterdam also because of a reason, tell this surgery to Vogeorge. Ava gives this surgery to her Was going to tell her when she saw her going towards the hospital, she called at the time, yet was in a hurry, she did not hear anything, then at the same time she once hit her from behind, because of this, she became uncoscious but fell. , the accident happened late that his nerves had been frozen for a while, some society was not coming that when Ava saw him for a while, he felt that, after all, what happened because Ava was just behind him and the other thing It was that the car was already driving on the wrong side, due to which Ava asked George several times to take care of her, but in a hurry, she did not even hear Ava's voice, but Ava also followed her, but seeing George's condition, she told him First went to Hospitlekar because her nerves were not moving, she was bleeding profusely from her head, so At that time Ava had gone to the camp and felt that whatever happened to George was the reason behind her as she had already made a wish to the parent that she would not kill Georgi. After a while she started to feel that her mother's hand was behind everything. But she clearly said that if I had to kill her, then why would she send you and wait for so long, if I had told, she could have killed her earlier. Leaving his relationship, he started telling him and one day he also told the parent that if Kishi looked after George again and tried to kill him, even if the fate would be his but the time would be mine and in his life only Lungi and Apne Aise Kabhi Kiya Toh I will forget what you look like to me.So just stay out of it from my love... Yeh toh kuchnahi hai abhi toh There is going to be a turning point that no one would have expected, that accident is not an accident, thanks to the fact that the car took the wrong side of the car to kill George and the person behind it took the lawyer to Marra Arjun to jail. ..ie George's dad did all this but why did he do it, what would be the reason ..and it doesn't end now when ava went to the hospital again but there were no doctors and neither was George He was kidnapped, he was killed..but let me tell you one thing Anurag was not behind everything...I didn't mean the work of his Fake Dad nor did the foster do anything after all who did what undefined ava joe George came to kill her, later she falls in love with her, foster sent her daughter to kill Jishnushe but she did not succeed and on the third side, how did Anurag know that George is not his son, and said that Anurag knew this

too. That he is not his beta, even then try to kill him because what for the property and the most important thing of family is What is the connection, how did his son die, is it really the same reason that everyone told, it is something else?????? I had said that no mystery may be one but its characters are many.

""Neither I have any intention, I am the moon of love, nor any dream. If I can find it, I will be able to find a lover, then society, but it is just a mystery or a coincidence.."

www.ingramcontent.com/pod-product-compliance
Lightning Source LLC
Chambersburg PA
CBHW031638170726
47990CB00017B/1544

9 798885 461313